For Max
who thinks sprouts
are yummy!

The SMELLY SPROUT © 2007
by Allan Plenderleith

All rights reserved.

First Published in this format in 2009
Reprinted in 2010
Ravette Publishing Limited
PO Box 876, Horsham, West Sussex RH12 9GH

ISBN: 978-1-84161-322-2

The Smelly Sprout

by Allan Plenderleith

RAVETTE PUBLISHING

It was Christmas day, Santa had been and all the presents were unwrapped.

The turkey was in the oven and Dad was helping Mum prepare the vegetables.

Broccoli, carrots, potatoes and peas.

Yummy!

But one vegetable had been overlooked.

There he lay, all alone, at the bottom
of the vegetable basket.

A little green sprout.

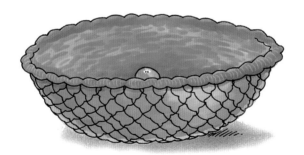

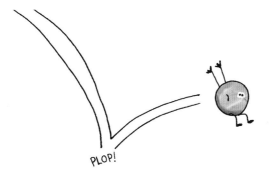

PLOP!

The sprout looked around and saw he was alone
so he decided to make himself known.

"Ahem! Excuse me!" he said in a tiny voice.
"I think you've forgotten about me."

I think it's safe to say that Mum and Dad
do not like sprouts.

The sprout stepped out into the big, wide world.

It was big. And quite wide too.

The streets were very quiet
and the shops were all closed.

Suddenly the little sprout felt very lonely indeed.

But then he saw something wonderful...

The little sprout climbed up
the tree to join the other
colourful balls.

Suddenly the tree began
to quiver and shake.

"Urgh!" said the tree.

"Something green and smelly is climbing up my branches!"

"It's a smelly sprout!" screeched one of the baubles.

Out, smelly sprout!

The little sprout came to a pretty street where the houses were decorated with colourful lights.

In every garden there was a snowman.

And on every snowman's face was a bright orange carrot.

All except one.

The snowman had no nose at all -
it had in fact been used in an emergency for
someone's Christmas dinner.

The sprout saw the little hole
on the snowman's face and thought
it looked like a lovely place to sit.

So he climbed up the snowman's cold body, passing its lumpy coal smile on the way, and sat down in the little hole.

Out, smelly sprout!

As he walked through the scary woods he could feel eyes all around, staring.

But then the sprout saw something...

It was a little mouse.

He looked very cold and sad.

"Hello," said the sprout.
"Are you alright?"

"I'm looking for food," shivered the mouse.
"I need to eat before I sleep for the winter."

The sprout was about to reply when...

Groowwwl!

"Was that your tummy?" asked the sprout.

"Er, I don't think so!" said the mouse.

The sprout and the mouse ran as fast as their little legs could carry them.

But the fox was fast too.

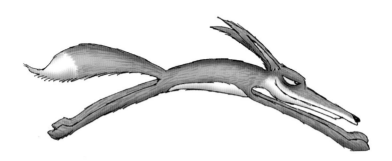

They ran through the icy twigs and
frosty bushes.

But all the time the fox
was close behind.

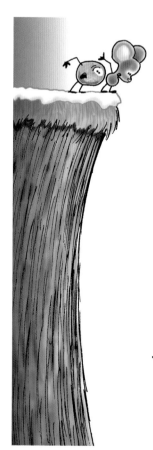

Suddenly the ground
disappeared before them.

They had nowhere to go.

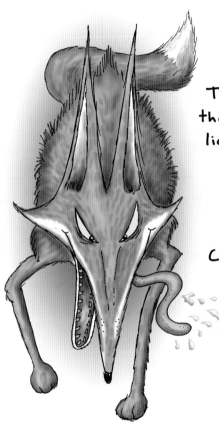

The fox came towards them, his slippery tongue licking his slobbery lips.

Sluuurrp!

"Time for my ChristMOUSE dinner!" drooled the fox.

But just as the fox was about to chomp...

...the little sprout jumped inside the fox's mouth!

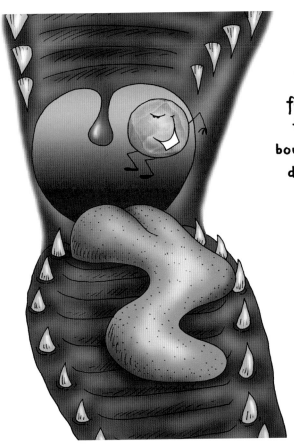

Inside the
fox's mouth
the sprout
bounced up and
down on his
tongue.

Boing!

Boing!

Boing!

"Urgh!" cried the fox. "A smelly sprout!
I hate smelly sprouts!"

I think it's safe to say that foxes
do not like sprouts.

Out, smelly sprout!

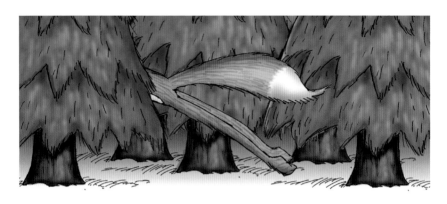

"Oh thankyou! Thankyou!" said the mouse.

The sprout was about to reply when...

"Was that your tummy?" asked the sprout.

"Er, yes it was actually," said the mouse.

"Then you must have ME for dinner!"
said the sprout.

"R..really?" said the mouse.

"Of course..." said the sprout.

Back in his cosy nest,
the mouse had a scrummy
Christmas dinner.

Afterwards, the mouse felt so full
he went straight to bed.

And the sprout was very happy
to have found a home at last...

...inside a nice warm tummy.